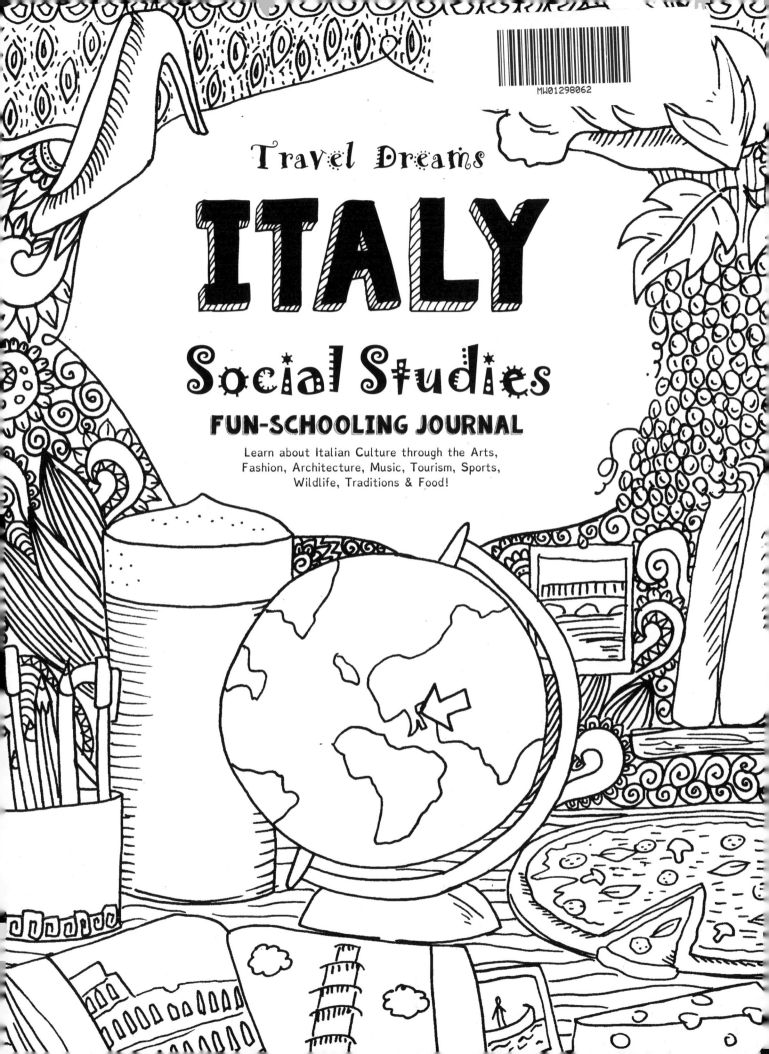

To hear traditional music from this country listen to

Travel Dreams Geography

AROUND THE WORLD IN 14 SONGS

Search for Amazon Product Number: B072C2QXJS

Around the world in 14 songs is a delightful musical tour of the world. Adults and children will enjoy these original instrumental songs that reflect the authentic style of music that originated on all six major continents. Travel to the rhythm and melody of traditional instruments, and enjoy the fun-filled tunes.

The musical journey begins in Ireland, sweeps across Europe, dances through Asia, Africa and then soars over the ocean to Australia and the Caribbean! After an exciting night at a Smoky Mountain bluegrass festival you will enjoy a siesta in Mexico and finally land in Brazil where you will join the festa in Rio-De-Janeiro.

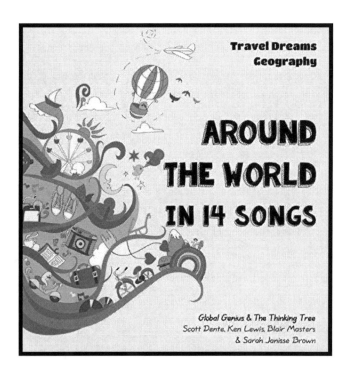

Music has never been more fun... or educational!

Travel Dreams
ITALY
FUN-SCHOOLING JOURNAL

An Adventurous Approach
Social Studies

Learn about Italian Culture Through the Arts, Fashion, Architecture, Music, Tourism, Sports, Wildlife, Traditions & Food!

Travel Dreams
ITALY
Fun-Schooling
Journal

Name:

Date:

Contact Information:

About Me:

The Thinking Tree LLC
Copyright 2016
Do Not Copy

Let's Learn!

Topics & Activities You Can Explore With This Curriculum:

- Ethnic Cooking
- Travel
- History of Interesting Places
- How People Live
- Tourism
- Transportation
- Wildlife and Natural Wonders
- Cultural Traditions
- Natural Disasters
- Famous and Interesting People
- Missionary Stories
- Scientific Discoveries
- Fashion
- Architecture
- Plants
- Animals
- Maps
- Language

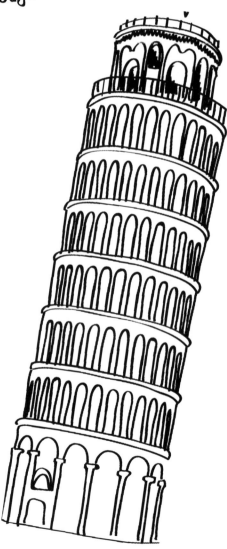

ITALY

Travel Dreams Fun-School Journal

You are going to learn about Italy

Teacher & Parent To-Do List:

- Plan a trip to Italy or just plan a trip to the library or local bookstore.
- Download Google Earth so your child can zoom in and learn more!
- Choose online videos about Italy so your child can learn about culture, food, tourism, traditions and history.
- Be prepared to help your child choose an ethnic recipe and shop for the ingredients.

Go to the Library or Bookstore to Pick Out:

- Books about Italy
- One Atlas or Book of Maps
- One Colorful Cookbook with Recipes from Italy

DRAW THE COVER OF YOUR BOOKS!

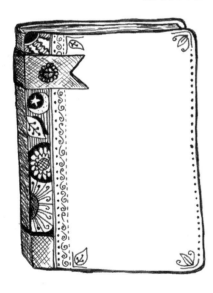  

COLOR IN ITALY ON THE MAP

Zoom into Italy using Google Earth and explore the wonders of this amazing country!

LABEL THE MAP
Add 15 Interesting Things to this Map!

Write or Draw
Use your Library Books

Popular Foods:	Traditional Clothing:
Draw the Flag:	A Quote or Proverb:
A Historic Event:	A Famous Landmark:

LEARNING TIME

READ A BOOK AND WATCH A VIDEO ABOUT FOOD IN ITALY:

BOOK TITLE: _____
_____
VIDEO TITLE: _____
_____
_____

What did you learn?
_____
_____
_____
_____
_____
_____

ITALIAN CUISINE

What do Italians love to eat?

Can you list **5** of the most popular Italian dishes?

1. _____
2. _____
3. _____
4. _____
5. _____

Draw your favorite Italian food

Find a Recipe From
ITALY

TITLE:

_____

Ingredients:

_____ _____

_____ _____

_____ _____

_____ _____

_____ _____

Instructions:

_____

_____

_____

_____

_____

_____

_____

_____

Step by Step Food Prep:

1	2
3	4
5	6

DRAW THE FOOD THAT YOU PREPARED!

RATE THE RESULTS! 1, 2, 3, 4, 5

Color the words that best describe your food:

DELICIOUS
YUMMY
TASTY
GREAT
DELIGHTFUL
OKAY
BLAH!
GROSS
YUCKY
DISGUSTING
STINKY
ICKY

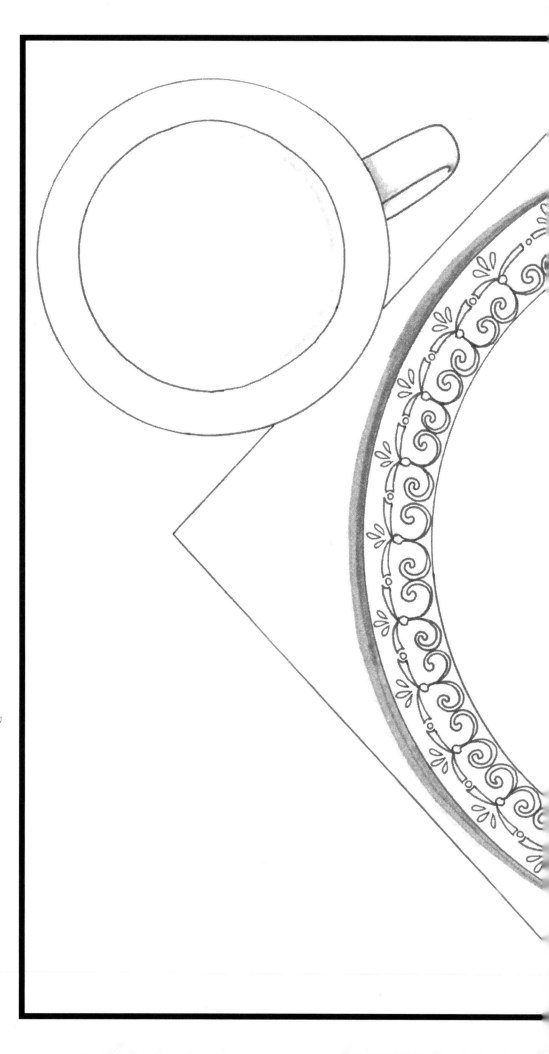

What to Do in Italy

Create a **COMIC STRIP** showing your dream adventure!

LEARNING TIME

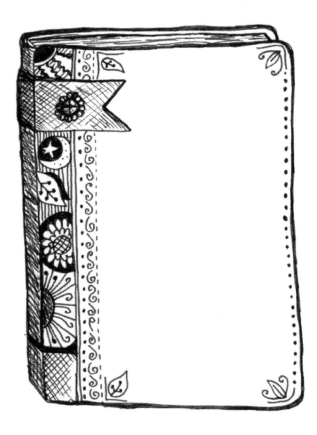

READ A BOOK AND WATCH A VIDEO ABOUT A FAMOUS PERSON

BOOK TITLE: _____
_____
VIDEO TITLE: _____
_____
_____

Write 3 Interesting Biography Facts
_____
_____
_____
_____
_____
_____

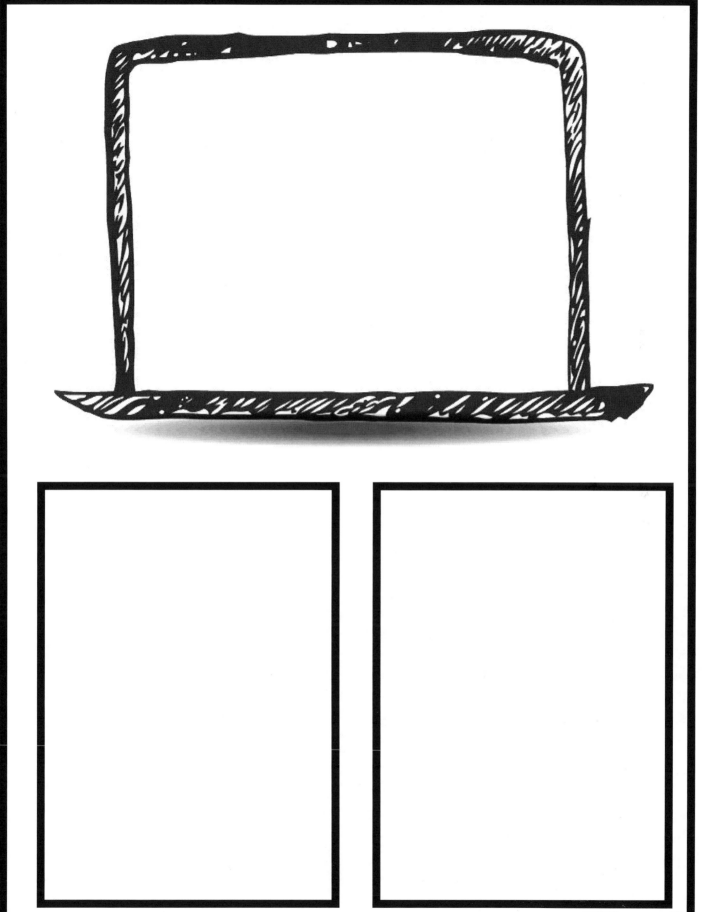

All About Style
ITALY
Fashion in the City

_____

_____

_____

MODERN STYLES
Draw yourself dressed like a stylish Italian:

Color The Traditional Costume:

Trace and color this traditional Female Italian costume

Trace and color this traditional male Italian costume

ITALIAN HISTORY

Write about a Historic Event

LEARNING TIME

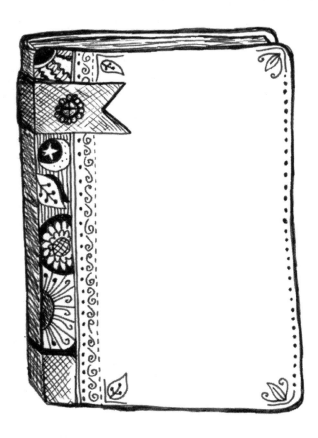

READ A BOOK AND WATCH A VIDEO ABOUT NATURE & WILDLIFE

BOOK TITLE: _____
_____
VIDEO TITLE: _____
_____
_____

Notes:

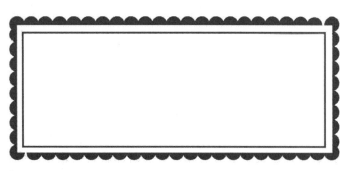

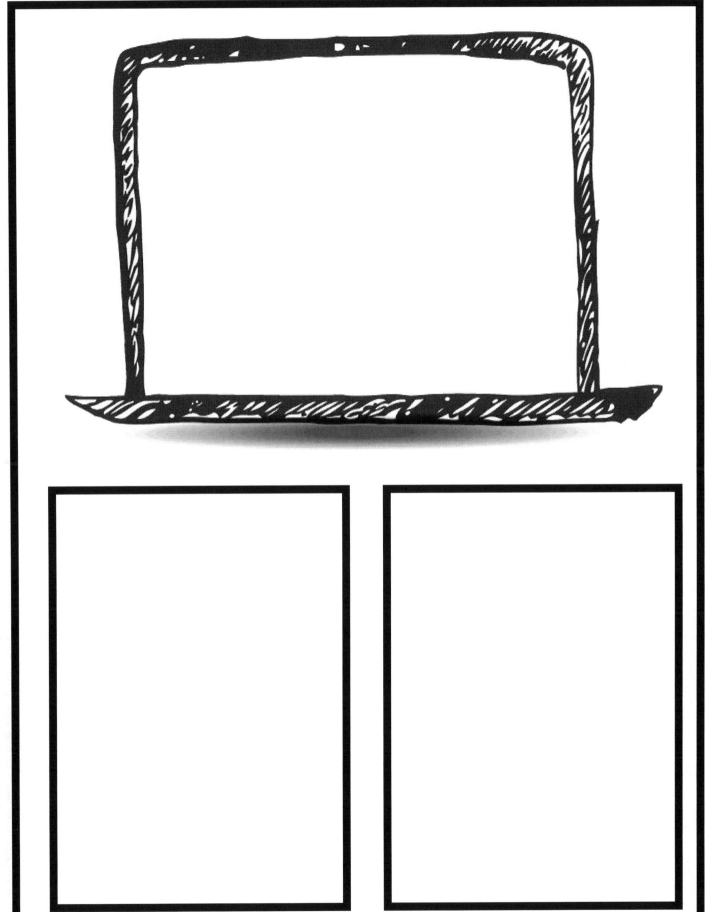

What Animals Live in Italy? Can you list ten?

1. _____
2. _____
3. _____
4. _____
5. _____
6. _____
7. _____
8. _____
9. _____
10. _____

Draw each of the animals

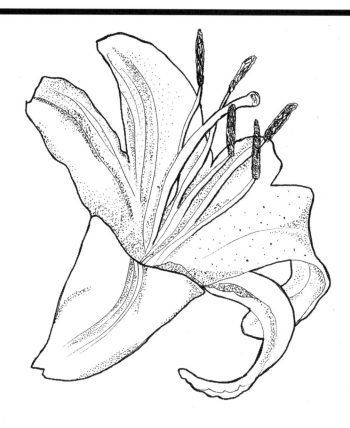

PLANTS IN ITALY

Can you list ten flowers or trees found in Italy?

1. _____
2. _____
3. _____
4. _____
5. _____
6. _____
7. _____
8. _____
9. _____
10. _____

Draw each of the plants

HISTORY OF MUSIC IN ITALY

Write about a famous Italian musician:

_____

_____
_____
_____
_____
_____
_____

What instrument did he/she play?

_____

Can you draw it?

A NATIONAL INSTRUMENT

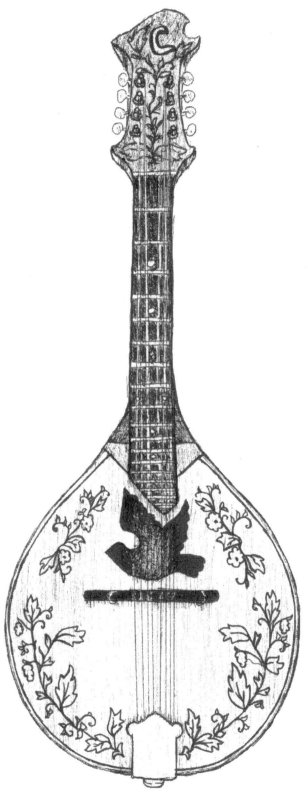

To hear traditional music from this country listen to
Travel Dreams Geography— Around the World in **14** Songs

Track Number & Song Name:
03-Italy - Lost in Venice

ITALIAN ART & ENTERTAINMENT

Read a book or watch a documentary about art and entertainment in Italy

Write down 5 interesting things you learned:

1. _____
2. _____
3. _____
4. _____
5. _____

Draw or doodle in Italian style

Write down a quote or a lyric from a famous Italian poem or song

HISTORY OF TRANSPORTATION IN ITALY

Find 3 interesting facts about Italian transportation

1. _____
   _____
   _____

2. _____
   _____
   _____

3. _____
   _____
   _____

Use your imagination and add something to this picture.

Write a short story about this picture

_____
_____
_____
_____
_____
_____
_____
_____

ITALIAN INVENTIONS

Read a book or watch a documentary about your favorite Italian inventor:

_____

Write down 5 interesting things about his/her life:

1. _____
2. _____
3. _____
4. _____
5. _____

Write down 3 Italian inventions that changed the world:

1. _____
2. _____
3. _____

Draw your Favorite Italian Invention

ITALIAN ATHLETES

Read a book or watch a documentary about your favorite Italian Athlete:

_____

Write down 5 interesting things about his/her life:

1. _____
2. _____
3. _____
4. _____
5. _____

Draw your Favorite Italian Sport

ITALIAN HOMES
Write about a family tradition in Italy

_____

_____

_____

_____

ITALIAN TRADITIONS
Draw some traditional Italian décor elements

Trace & Color
A TRADITIONAL ITALIAN HOME

Design Your Own
ITALIAN HOME

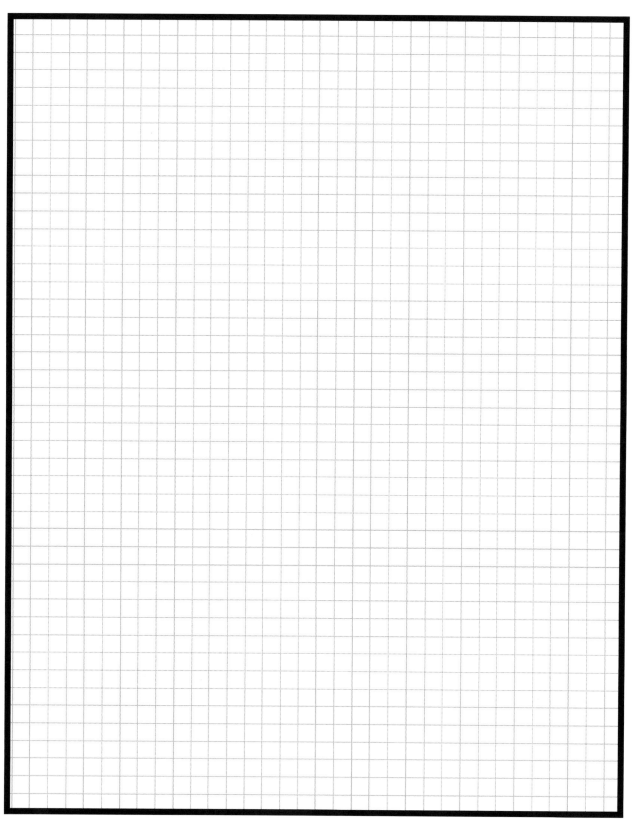

Find and color in the hidden objects

LEARNING TIME

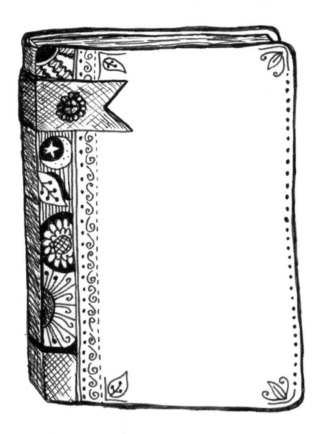

READ A BOOK AND WATCH A VIDEO ABOUT TOURISM & TRAVEL

BOOK TITLE: _____
_____
VIDEO TITLE: _____
_____
_____

Notes:

PLAN A TRIP TO THE CAPITAL OF ITALY

Who are you going with?

What are you taking with you?

How long is your trip?

What do you want to see or visit?

PLAN YOUR TRIP
What to Do in ROME

Five Things to Know when Traveling to ITALY

1 _____

2 _____

3 _____

4 _____

5 _____

What to Say

Create a **COMIC STRIP** using six Italian words or phrases:

59

CREATIVE WRITING

Write a story about an imaginary trip to Italy

Illustrate your Story

Do It Yourself HOMESCHOOL JOURNALS

BY THE THINKING TREE, LLC

Copyright Information

This Journal, and electronic printable downloads are for personal use only. If you purchase individual workbooks for each child, the curriculum may be used in schools or co-ops.

For Family Use:

You may make copies of these materials for only the children in your household.

All other uses of this material must be permitted in writing by the Thinking Tree LLC. It is a violation of copyright law to distribute the electronic files or make copies for your friends, associates or students without our permission.

For information on using these materials for businesses, co-ops, summer camps, day camps, daycare, afterschool program, churches, or schools please contact us for licensing.

FunSchoolingBooks.com

DyslexiaGames.com

Contact Us: jbrown@DyslexiaGames.com

Made in the USA
Columbia, SC
26 July 2024